Jesus Blesses the Children

Mark 10:13–16 for children

Written by Gloria Truitt
Illustrated by Kathy Mitter

ARCH® Books
Copyright © 1996 Concordia Publishing House
3558 S. Jefferson Avenue, St. Louis, MO 63118-3968
Manufactured in the United States of America

During the time when Jesus preached
Throughout the holy land,
People came from far and wide
To hear His words firsthand.

Some mothers brought young children, and
As little hands they clutched,
Hoped that by their Master their
Young children would be touched.

But Christ's disciples frowned and said,
"Now children, go away!
The Lord cannot be bothered with
Young children—not today!"

They said that Jesus had no time
For children, young and small,
'Cause they were not important—
They were children after all!

To His disciples Jesus said,
"Do not get in their way.
Let the children come to Me.
I tell you, let them stay.

"Believe Me, God loves *every* child—
To God they *all* belong.
If you think differently, My friends,
Then you are very wrong.

"Now listen, for I tell the truth—
I would not tell you lies—
God's kingdom includes every one
Of every age and size."

And to the grown-ups in the crowd
He said, "Don't doubt and grumble.
God's kingdom will be yours if you
Have childlike faith so humble."

When Jesus spoke those caring words,
The little children stayed,
Then went to Jesus, full of trust—
They weren't a bit afraid.

When Jesus took them in His arms,
He patted them and smiled,
Then lovingly He blessed them as
He prayed for each young child.

What would you say to Jesus if
He came to visit you?
Would you smile and welcome Him
And say, "How do you do?"

Now if you really knew He was
The Lord to whom you pray,
I'm sure you'd thank Him for the things
He gives you every day—

Like sun and rain to make plants grow,
And loving folks who care;
For food and clothes and cuddly pets
And friends who say, "Let's share!"

Because I'm blessed by Jesus—
And this I surely know—
He will *always* love me, and
Protect me as I grow.

I love my Lord and Savior—
I pray to Him each day—
And if He came to visit me,
These are the things I'd say:

Dear Parents:

As you talk with your child about this book, explain that Jesus loves all people—big and small. God chose your child to be His own in Baptism, and will continue to strengthen your child's faith through the guidance of His Holy Spirit.

Talk and pray with your child about some ways you might share Jesus' love with others. You could invite a neighborhood friend to Sunday school, make a family banner about Jesus to display, include school friends invited for sleepovers in family devotions. Thank Jesus for loving you and keeping you close to Him.

The Editor

The Arch® Book Bible Story Library

Bible Beginnings

9-1114	The World God Made
9-1496	The Story of Creation
9-1486	The Fall into Sin
9-1110	The Story of Noah's Ark
9-1294	Noah and God's Promises

People of the Old Testament

9-1502	Abraham's Big Test
9-1494	Joseph Forgives His Brothers
9-1158	The Princess and the Baby
9-1291	Moses and the 10 Plagues
9-1454	Caleb, God's Special Spy
9-1465	Samson
9-1458	Samuel and the Wake-up Call
9-1457	David and Goliath
9-1116	The Boy with a Sling
9-1434	David and Jonathan
9-1194	The Queen Who Saved Her People
9-1136	The Man Caught by a Fish
9-1466	Three Men in a Fiery Furnace
9-1127	Daniel in the Lions' Den
9-1498	Daniel and the Roaring Lions

Places of the Old Testament

9-1473	The Fall of Jericho
9-1135	The Walls Came Tumbling Down

Christmas Arch® Books

9-1442	God Promised Us a Savior
9-1499	Mary's Christmas Story
9-1140	Mary's Story
9-1467	Baby Jesus Is Born
9-1118	The Baby Born in a Stable
9-1488	My Merry Christmas Arch® Book
9-1213	The Night the Angels Sang
9-1497	Three Presents for Baby Jesus
9-1439	The Visit of the Wise Men

Parables and Lessons of Jesus

9-1475	The Kind Samaritan
9-1102	The Good Samaritan
9-1275	The Father Who Forgave
9-1495	The Prodigal Son
9-1209	The Seeds That Grew to Be a Hundred
9-1309	The Parables of Jesus
9-1106	Jon and the Little Lost Lamb
9-1441	Jesus the Good Shepherd
9-1500	Jesus Blesses the Children
9-1210	The Day the Little Children Came

Miracles Jesus Performed

59-1503	The Story of Jesus' Baptism and Temptation
59-1445	Jesus' First Miracle
59-1138	The Boy Who Gave His Lunch Away
59-1111	The Little Boat That Almost Sank
59-1474	Jesus Walks on the Water
59-1468	Jesus Calms the Storm
59-1221	He Remembered to Say Thank You
59-1485	Jesus and Bartimaeus

Easter Arch® Books

59-1455	Jesus Enters Jerusalem
59-1501	The Very First Lord's Supper
59-1245	The Bread and the Wine
59-1451	Good Friday
59-1242	The Man Who Carried the Cross for Jesus
59-1493	My Happy Easter Arch® Book
59-1431	The Easter Women
59-1504	Thomas, the Doubting Disciple
59-1139	The Fishermen's Surprise
59-1476	Jesus Returns to Heaven
59-1452	The Coming of the Holy Spirit

People of the New Testament

59-1307	Jesus' 12 Disciples
59-1460	Zacchaeus
59-1293	Jesus Forgives Peter

Arch® Book Companion Series

59-1301	God, I've Gotta Talk to You
59-1315	God, I've Gotta Talk to You Again
59-1459	The Lord's Prayer
59-1314	The Greatest Gift Is Love
59-1487	My Happy Birthday Book

PassAlong Arch® Books

59-1463	God's Good Creation
59-1464	Noah's Floating Zoo
59-1469	Baby Moses' River Ride
59-1478	Moses and the Freedom Flight
59-1484	Journey to the Promised Land
59-1483	David and the Dreadful Giant
59-1470	Jonah's Fishy Adventure
59-1477	Daniel in the Dangerous Den
59-1471	Baby Jesus, Prince of Peace
59-1481	Jesus and the Little Children
59-1482	Jesus and the Grumpy Little Man
59-1472	Jesus' Big Picnic
59-1462	Jesus Stills the Storm
59-1479	Jesus and Jairus' Little Girl
59-1461	God's Easter Plan
59-1480	Peter and the Biggest Birthday

More than 55 million sold!

For more than 25 years, Arch® Books have captivated children ages 5–9. Each book presents a complete Bible story through colorful illustrations and fun-to-read rhymes.

The Arch Book series includes more than 100 titles covering key Bible stories and themes from Genesis through Acts. Start your Arch Book library today!

Also, enjoy your favorite Arch Books on audiocassette with Arch Books Aloud!®

9 780570 075271

CPH®
Concordia Publishing House

CH
59-1500
ISBN 0-570-07527-0